The Wishing Stone

#2 Dragon Dilemma

By: Lorana Hoopes

Illustrated by: Kendall "Mavis" Jackson

DEDICATION

This book is dedicated first and foremost to my children who are the characters and inspiration for my stories and then to all the young readers out there looking for a good story. I hope you enjoy reading this book as much I enjoyed writing it.

CONTENTS

ACKNOWLEDGMENTS

Thank you to the wonderful moms and kids who beta read this for me and let me know they enjoyed it. Thank you Kathy, Joann, Natalie, Misty, Amber, Kim, and everyone who read.

Be sure to visit https://twoheartbeats.org to get a free audio reading of the first chapter of this book from author Lorana Hoopes

1 THE TROUBLE WITH SIBLINGS

Spenser stared at the clock on the wall, willing it to be 3:15. He couldn't wait to go home and try out his wishing stone again. He had only gotten to use it once since receiving it, and he was aching to try it again.

A week ago, Spenser had come across a mysterious stranger on his way home from school. The man, after hearing that Spenser didn't like to read, had offered him a white stone. The man had said that magical things would happen when Spenser held the stone while reading.

Spenser hadn't believed the mysterious stranger at first, but then Spenser had held the stone and wished to meet Arco, the character in the book he had been reading, and had been transported back to dinosaur time, where he got to see a T-rex up close. That had been amazing.

Since then, he had been begging his mother to take him back to the library to get another book. Finally, yesterday, she had agreed, and at home on his bed right now was Merlin and the Dragon. Spenser loved magic and dragons, so he was excited not only to read this book but to visit Merlin himself.

The bell finally rang and Spenser bounded out of his seat. He slung his backpack over his shoulders and headed for the door.

"Hey, you want to ride bikes?" his friend Zane asked.

Spenser was torn. He did want to ride bikes and he had just gotten a new bike for Christmas, but he really wanted to try the stone again. It was in his pocket right now, and his fingers itched to touch it.

"I can't tonight, but do you want to ride tomorrow?"

Zane's face grew sad for a moment before lighting up at the prospect of a meeting tomorrow. "Sure, that will be fun."

Spenser waved goodbye and started towards home. He didn't live very far, so he walked to and from school. The path went through a little park and kept him away from the streets. Every day, he kept his eyes peeled for the mysterious stranger. He hadn't seen him again, but he hoped to. For one, he wanted to thank the man for the magical rock, but he also wanted to see if the man had any other magical items.

There was no luck today, either. He did not spot the man on his walk home.

Spenser opened the green front door of his house and called out to his mother. "Mom, I'm home."

"In the kitchen, honey," came her reply.

He tossed his backpack by the door and headed that way, but before he had even rounded the corner, Kayleigh appeared, hugging his legs.

"Brudder," she said, smiling up at him.

"Hi, Kayleigh. Did you have a fun day today?"

"Yesh," she said, her little blond head nodding up and down.

When she finally released his leg, he continued into the kitchen. His mother sat at the table with Jackson, showing him how to write the letter D.

"Spenser, look," Jackson said, holding up his picture. "D is for dragon." Jackson was just as fascinated by dragons as Spenser was.

"It's nice," Spenser said. His hand patted his pocket. How much longer would he have to stay down here before he could sneak up to his room?

"Do you have homework, Spenser?" his mother asked.

This was his chance. "Just some reading, mom. Can I go upstairs to read?"

"Sure," his mother agreed. "I'll call you when it's time for dinner."

Barely able to contain his excitement, Spenser turned around and bounded up the stairs.

He threw open his door. The book called to him from his bed, and in his haste, he forgot to shut the door behind him. Climbing up on the bed, he sat cross legged, his back to the door, and opened the book.

He didn't see Jackson and Kayleigh sneak into the room behind him.

"Merlin was a wise old wizard," Spenser read aloud, "but could he find a way to tame the fierce dragon that was terrorizing the people in King Egeus's castle?" Spenser pulled out the stone. "I wish I could help Merlin."

The tingling shot up his arm, and the room began to fade.

When the tingling stopped, Spenser found himself standing on the stone floor of a large grey room.

"Is this a castle?" Jackson asked.

Spenser whirled around to find Jackson and Kayleigh in the room with him.

"How did you get here?" Spenser asked, his hands on his waist. He was careful to keep his voice quiet.

"We grabbed your shirt when you started to shimmer," Jackson said. "Where are we?"

"Shh! We're in King Egeus's castle. Merlin is around here somewhere trying to figure out how to tame a dragon."

"Merwin," Kayleigh said clapping. "Dragon? Where is he?"

"I guess we better find out," Spenser sighed. This might be a little tougher with his brother and sister tagging along, but on the other hand, it was nice to have someone to share the experience with. "Come with me, but be quiet."

2 MEETING THE KING

After leaving the small room they had landed in, the trio sneaked down the stone hallway. The small cracks in the brick layering allowed cold air to seep in and Spenser shivered as they walked. At the end of the hallway was a large oak door.

"Should we open it?" Jackson asked.

"I think we have to," Spenser said, shrugging his shoulders.

"Yesh," Kaylie said placing her little hands against the door.

Spenser and Jackson joined her and pushed on the heavy door. With the help of all three, the door began to open. T

Though he expected a loud squeaking, the door swung open with barely a whisper.

A large room opened before them. There was a grand wooden table and chairs. Beautiful paintings and tapestries hung along the walls. At the head of the table, an older man with a long white beard and a purple robe was talking to another man wearing a long red cape and golden crown. He too had a beard, but it was shorter and a dark brown color similar to their father's beard.

"It's Merlin and the king," Spenser whispered.

Jackson and Kayleigh simply stared wide-eyed.

"We have to do something," King Egeus said. "The dragon is terrorizing the children."

"I know, sir, but I don't know what else to do. My magic hasn't worked. It just seems to make him angrier."

"Perhaps we can help," Spenser said, stepping forward.

The two men turned to the three children.

"Who are you?" King Egeus asked. His eyes darted to the left and right for his guards as if he feared an attack.

"I'm Spenser, and this is my brother, Jackson, and my sister, Kayleigh."

"Hi," Kayleigh waved.

"How did you get here?" Merlin asked. "What kind of magic is this?"

"We used a magic stone, a wishing stone," Spenser said.

"I've never heard of such a thing," Merlin said, stepping closer to them.

"Show him," Jackson said as he nudged Spenser.

Spenser shot Jackson a dirty look, but pulled the stone from his pocket. "I'll show you, but you can't take it or we won't be able to get home." He held out his hand and Merlin leaned in even further to examine the stone.

"It looks harmless enough," Merlin said to the king.

"That's good, but how exactly do you expect to help us?" the king asked. "Does that magic stone tame dragons?"

"I don't think so," Spenser said, "but it's only my second time using it, so I'm not really sure."

"So, how do you expect to help us out?" Merlin asked.

"Well, sometimes the solution is as simple as seeing something through someone else's eyes," Spenser said. "Is there a way we can see the dragon?"

"Yesh, dragon," Kayleigh screamed as she clapped her hands and bounced up and down.

"I suppose they could observe from the courtyard," Merlin said to Egeus. "The dragon usually comes around after noonday meal."

"You can observe, but do not approach the dragon," Egeus said. "I have a hard enough time keeping our children safe. I do not want to responsible for you as well."

"We will just look sir, for now," Spenser said.

The king nodded and then turned to one of the open windows in the room.

"Follow me," Merlin said.

He led them back out of the room and down the grey hall. Instead of returning to the room they had arrived in, he turned left down a hallway and into a gaping room with a raised ceiling. A black chandelier that held five candles hung from the high ceiling.

On the left was a large brick opening. As three black pots hung over it, Spenser assumed it was the stove of the time. Though he hadn't cooked much on his stove at home, he could imagine how much harder this would be. A recess in the wall held a large stack of firewood and a long wooden table sat in the middle of the room.

"Is this the kitchen?" asked Spenser.

"Of course," Merlin answered smiling. "This is my favorite room in the whole castle. Perhaps you can stay and join us tonight for some bread, beef stew, and salted olives."

Jackson scrunched up his face. "Salted olives? Yuck."

"Oh no, sir, they are very delicious. Just you wait and see," Merlin said.

Merlin crossed out of the kitchen and into another large room with a high ceiling. A long table filled this room, though the small windows didn't let in much light.

"This is the Great Hall," Merlin said. "When we have lots visitors, we eat here. The more important you are, the closer you get to sit to the king."

"So, I guess those seats meant you weren't very important," Spenser said, pointing to the wooden benches at the farthest side of the room.

"Well, not everyone can sit next to the king," Merlin said.

Leaving the Great Hall, they entered a large open space. Here children were playing games that resembled the chess set Spenser had gotten for his birthday and playing with crude dolls. Women in long dresses hung laundry on a long line that stretched across the yard.

"This is the courtyard," Merlin said gesturing to the open space. "It is here where the dragon comes every day. He scares the children inside and then clomps around on the bricks."

Just then a large thwap thwap thwap sounded.

"What is that?" Jackson asked.

Spenser looked up to the sky just as a large red shape flew overhead.

"It's the dragon," a woman screamed. "Hurry inside."

A flurry of activity surrounded the trio as children grabbed their games and ran past them. The women followed, scooping up any stragglers. Merlin grabbed Jackson's and Kayleigh's hands and began to pull them back to the Great Hall.

"Come on, Spenser," he called.

The shape passed overhead one more time, and Spenser turned and ran.

3 RARE AS RUBY

Once they were all safely in the Great Hall, Jackson, Kayleigh, and Spenser peered out of the entrance way. An enormous red dragon landed in the now empty courtyard. Its scales sparkled like rubies in the sun and on its head were two gold horns. The dragon's talon-like nails clacked on the cobblestones as it walked about. Its large gold eye looked into the small windows and doors, but its head was far too massive to fit in.

After circling the courtyard once, the dragon sat back on its haunches (hind legs) and let out a loud wail. The giant head turned to the sky and an enormous blue flame shot out of the dragon's mouth. Then the dragon laid its head on the stones.

"The dragon sounded almost sad," Spenser mused aloud.

"Spenser, can I see the stone?" Jackson asked.

"Not now, Jackson," Spenser said. "I'm trying to figure out a way to help."

"That's just it though," Jackson said, "I have a feeling. Please just let me hold the stone a second? I'll give it right back."

"Fine," Spenser sighed and reached into his pocket. He pulled out the smooth white stone and held it out to Jackson. "You better be careful not to lose it, or we can't get home," he said.

"I won't lose it," Jackson said, wrinkling his nose. He hated it when Spenser bossed him around.

Spenser placed the stone in his palm and Jackson felt a tingle run up his arm.

"Why won't anyone play with me?" a voice said.

Jackson looked at Spenser who was staring back at him with wide eyes.

"Every time, they run away. I'm not scary."

"Who is that?" Spenser and Merlin asked together.

With wide eyes, Jackson looked to the giant red creature in the courtyard. Were they hearing the dragon?

"How can I tell them I'm a nice dragon? I don't eat people. I don't even like meat."

"Spenser, I hear the dragon," Jackson said excitedly. "It's not a mean dragon at all. It just wants to play."

"I know. I hear it too," Spenser said. "How come I can't hear the dragon when I hold the stone?"

"Perhaps the stone grants different powers to each of you," Merlin suggested from behind them.

"So, when I hold it, we can understand animals?" Jackson asked.

"It would appear so," Merlin said.

"No, Kayleigh," Spenser yelled.

While Merlin and the boys had been discussing, Kayleigh had slipped out of the doorway and was now approaching the dragon. Her blond hair shimmered in the sunlight. The enormity of the dragon made her appear even smaller, but she walked with purpose.

"If the dragon eats her, mom is going to kill us," Jackson said.

"Shh, let's listen in," Spenser said, holding his finger to his mouth.

"What's this? A little girl who's not afraid of me?" The dragon's head turned ever so slightly toward Kayleigh. The movement was slow as if the dragon were afraid of scaring her away with quick movements.

Kayleigh continued to approach, her little hand held out the same way she approached dogs, giving them a chance to sniff her.

"I can create a protection spell," Merlin said, wringing his hands together nervously, "but I'll need a few minutes."

"No, it's okay," Jackson said, shaking his head. "The dragon is just curious about her."

Jackson, Spenser, and Merlin watched with baited breath as Kayleigh reached the dragon.

"Hi, dragon," her little voice carried back to them. She reached up her hand and touched the dragon's nose.

The dragon's lips pulled back into an almost smile and it puffed out its nostrils sending Kayleigh stumbling back a few feet. Spenser and Jackson rushed to her side and helped her up, forgetting their fear of the dragon for a moment.

"Oh no, did I hurt her?" the dragon's voice filled Jackson's head.

"It's okay," Jackson told the dragon. "You didn't mean it. You just have to be careful with your size. You are so much bigger."

The dragon's eyes widened. "You can hear me?"

"We all can as long as I hold the stone," Jackson said, nodding. "We want to be friends, but you have to be more careful."

"I will."

"Yesh, pwease," Kayleigh said, rubbing her bottom.

"Is it okay to touch it?" Spenser asked.

"I'm a female dragon. My name is Ruby. Please don't call me it."

"Sorry," Spenser said. The boys each grabbed one of Kayleigh's hands and they walked back to the dragon.

Spenser laid his hand on the scales. They were hard like how he imagined a suit of armor would be, but textured like a snake. "Wow," Spenser said as he ran his hand down the dragon. Her feet were nearly the size of Spenser. "It's okay," Spenser called to Merlin and the other children. "She's nice."

Slowly, the other children and the women stepped into the courtyard. When they finally accepted the dragon was not dangerous, they quickly surrounded her and began petting her much like a dog.

"Would they like a ride?"

Hands shot up all around and two or three at a time, the children climbed up on her back. They wrapped their arms around her golden horns and Ruby gently lifted off from the ground. After a few circles up in the air, she would return to the courtyard and the children would slide off her back, grinning from ear to ear.

Finally, it was Spenser, Jackson, and Kayleigh's turn. The boys helped Kayleigh up and then climbed up behind her. Jackson was careful to keep the stone clasped tightly in his left hand as he wrapped his right around the horn.

The thwap, thwap, thwap of her wings began and the ground grew more distant as they rose in the air. From this position, the trio could see the whole country side. A large moat circled the castle, but to the left of the castle, lush green grass spanned for quite a distance until it reached a forest of tall trees. To the right of the castle was another grassy area and another castle far in the distance. Behind the castle was a set of rocky cliffs that overlooked a clear blue body of water, and in front of the castle was another grassy plain but it led to a dark and foreboding forest.

"What is that place?" Jackson asked, pointing to the dark forest.

"That is the Forest of Shadows," Ruby answered. "I lost my sister in there. I need to go back to try and find her, but I'm not brave enough to go alone. That's why I was coming to the castle. I love the children, but I was also hoping to find a brave knight to accompany me."

"We'll help you," Jackson said.

Moments later, Ruby returned to the stone courtyard and the trio slid off her back.

"Wait here," Jackson told her. Ruby nodded and then laid her head down on the stones.

"What are you doing?" Spenser asked.

"She needs our help," Jackson said. His eyes scanned the courtyard for Merlin. When he finally spotted Merlin, he took off running. Spenser grabbed Kayleigh's hand and followed.

"Merlin," Jackson said, trying to catch his breath. "The dragon needs our help. She lost her sister in the Forest of Shadows, and she needs a brave knight to go in there with her.

Merlin's bushy white eyebrows creased together. "The Forest of Shadows is a very dangerous place. It's not for children."

"You said you could do a protection spell, right?" Spenser asked.

"I can, but I don't know if I could protect everyone at once or how long it would last. Let's discuss the matter with King Egeus over supper. It is about that time.

"Yesh hungry," Kayleigh spoke up, patting her tummy. "Can I have gowdfish?"

"Of course you can have fish if they caught any today," Merlin said as he led the way back into the Great Hall.

4 THE DINNER

The room was bustling with people bringing plates to the table. The candles in the overhead chandeliers had been lit as the sun was now beginning to set. Many people filled the table, but there were six empty chairs near the head of the table.

"It seems the king has deemed you important guests," Merlin said as he pointed their chairs out to them. Just as they were about to sit down, the King and Queen entered and walked to the head of the table. She was a beautiful woman with long golden hair and blue eyes.

"Oh, what sweet children," she said looking at each of them, though her eyes stayed longer on Kayleigh.

"You may sit down," King Egeus announced as he sat in his own chair.

Jackson and Spenser took two chairs on the King's right. Kayleigh sat closest to the King, but Spenser had to help her climb up onto the large wooden chair, and even then she could still barely reach the table.

Servants entered and began placing plates of food in front of each person, starting with the king, of course.

A bowl of a thin brown soup was placed in front of each of the children, followed by a hard, lumpy bread.

Kayleigh turned her big blue eyes on Spenser. "Brudder, can we eat this?"

Spenser shrugged and waited for the King to eat. He wasn't sure what the protocol was, but he assumed it would be proper to wait for the King.

When the King picked up his spoon, Spenser did the same. Steam rose from the broth, but the smell made Spenser's nose wrinkle. He took a tentative sip and nearly spit it back out. The broth was hot and full of spices. Spenser wasn't a fan of pepper, and he was pretty sure the broth was filled with it and cinnamon. An odd combination.*

Kayleigh took a tentative sip beside him and spat hers back in her bowl. Her eyes watered and she opened her mouth to wail.

"Take a sip," Spenser said, handing her the cup in front of her. A white liquid was inside, and he hoped it was milk.

She took a large sip of the drink and made a face, but at least she didn't spit it out. Jackson didn't even try the broth; he took a large bite of the bread instead.

"It's very hard," he said as he continued chewing.

Spenser and Kayleigh tried the bread as well and found it hard as well. Not knowing it was probably rude, Kayleigh tore off a hunk and dropped it in her milk. When it had soaked a few minutes, she pulled it out and bit off a piece.

"Better," she said smiling.

Thankfully, the other guests were so focused on their food that they weren't paying much attention to the three children.

After the king finished his broth, the bowls were removed and another course was brought in. This was a meat of some kind. Though Spenser didn't know what kind, the meat was edible. Then a course with some beans and vegetables came in. Spenser was full from the meat and it seemed Kayleigh and Jackson were as well because they pushed the food around on their plate.

When Kayleigh yawned, Merlin offered to excuse the children and show them to the room they would be sleeping in for the night.

"But we have to tell the king about the dragon," Jackson said.

"What about the dragon?" the king asked.

"We found out what she wants," Jackson said. "She is just looking for her sister, and she needs help. Her sister is lost in the Forest of Shadows."

"That is no place for children," the king said. "Why don't you get some sleep for tonight, and we'll discuss it in the morning."

The children nodded, as sleep was quickly creeping in on them. They followed Merlin out of the Great Hall. through several winding hallways, and into a spacious room with one large bed. A pole extended from each corner of the bed and fabric draped between the poles.

"What is that?" Jackson asked pointing at the fabric.

"That's a canopy," Merlin said.*

"We have to sleep together?" Spenser asked.

"Of course, that is how it's done," Merlin said. "Besides it will keep you warm. I will light the fireplace, but it might still get cold. Also, there's a chamberpot* under the bed if you need."

"What's a chamberpot?" Jackson asked.

"Well, it's our . . . you use it if you need the bathroom in the middle of the night," Merlin answered, his face coloring with a pink blush.

"You mean we pee in a pot?" Jackson asked again.

"Yes, and you can throw it out the window or we will get it in the morning," Merlin said.

"Ew," Kayleigh said.

"What do you have in your world?" Merlin asked.

"Toilets that flush," Spenser said.

"Toilets that flush. Amazing," Merlin said. "I wish I could see your world."

"Well, maybe you can come back with us," Spenser offered. "Merlin, I think we should go help Ruby in the morning. If you come with us, I'm sure we will be fine."

"We'll see," Merlin smiled. "I'll come by and check on you in the morning."

Merlin left the room, and the three children climbed into bed.

"I think we may need to help Ruby ourselves," Spenser said as he laid back on the pillow. "I don't think they're going to help us."

Jackson mumbled something sleepily, but Spenser couldn't make it out and his own eyes closed before he could ask Jackson to repeat it.

5 AWAKE TO ADVENTURE

The light spilling in the small window woke Spenser the next morning. He blinked a few times before looking over at Kayleigh and Jackson. He was surprised Jackson was still sleeping because at home he was usually the first one up in the mornings.

"Guys," Spenser whispered. He wasn't sure why he was whispering, whether it was to not startle them or because he was afraid someone might hear their plan.

Kayleigh opened her eyes first. "Bunny?" she asked, looking around for her favorite stuffed animal.

"Bunny is back at the house," Spenser said. He saw her blue eyes filling with tears and quickly continued. "Look, we just need to help Ruby today, and then we can go back home, okay?"

She looked at him for a moment, and then her small voice said, "Otay."

Jackson's hazel eyes popped open next. "Where are we?" he yawned.

"The castle, remember?" Spenser said, sitting up in the bed. "We have to go help Ruby."

"Shouldn't we wait for Merlin?" Jackson asked.

"I don't think they are going to help us," Spenser said.

"But we can't go in alone," Jackson said. "They said it was dangerous."

Spenser shrugged. "I don't know why, but I have the feeling the stone will protect us."

It took a little more convincing, but finally Jackson and Kayleigh agreed to go with him. They climbed out of the large bed and retrieved their shoes from the foot of the bed, where they had placed them last night.

After a few wrong turns, they found their way back out to the courtyard. Ruby lay curled in the far corner.

"I can't believe she stayed," Jackson said.

"Ruby," Kayleigh called and hurried toward the dragon.

At the sound of Kayleigh's voice, the dragon's eyes opened.

"Hand me the stone," Jackson said, and Spenser placed it in his hand.

"Good morning children."

"Good morning, Ruby," Jackson answered. "We're here to help you."

Ruby's head rose and she looked around the courtyard.

"Where are the brave knights?" she asked.

"We are the knights," Spenser said. He pulled back his shoulders, attempting to stretch himself as tall as he could.

The dragon shook her head slowly. "It is too dangerous for children."

"Spenser doesn't think the knights will help," Jackson answered her.

"Please," Spenser took a step closer to the red beast, "Let us help you."

Ruby seemed torn as the minutes stretched on before she finally nodded her head and lowered it down so the kids could climb aboard.

Jackson tucked the stone in the pocket of his jeans as he climbed up behind Spenser and Kayleigh. He definitely did not want to lose that.

Once all three had a hold on Ruby's horns, she flapped her mighty wings and lifted them off the stone ground. She flew over the castle walls and down towards the dark forest, landing just outside the entrance.

Jackson, Spenser, and Kayleigh all felt a chill as they tried to peer into the dark forest.

"Ruby wants us to stay on her back," Jackson told his brother and sister, who nodded silently.

The dragon paused for a moment and then cautiously began stepping into the darkened area. Trees with trunks more gray than brown rose all around them, and while the trees held leaves, they were too far up to determine the color. The thick leaves did block out a lot of the sunlight, however, which was why the forest was so dark.

As Ruby stepped farther into the forest, Spenser strained his ears to listen for sounds, but the air was still. There were no birds, no rustling of leaves, just silence. He shivered at the odd feeling in this forest. Suddenly, he felt like they were being watched. Looking deeper into the trees he was startled to see a pair of eyes looking back at him. The rest of the face slowly emerged and then a girl, carrying a bow floated out from behind the tree.

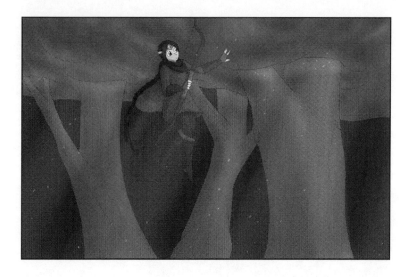

"Oh wow," she said, her voice full of excitement. "It really is a dragon. How do you do? I'm Gabriella, and I'm a huge fan. In fact, would you mind if I sketched you? I know I have some paper and charcoal in here somewhere."

She pulled a pack off her back and began rummaging through it, still talking to herself. "Ointment? Nope, that only helps with burns. Figs? No, but I'll want those for later. They make a great afternoon snack, you know? Oh, here it is."

She pulled out a rectangular whitish object and a black stick. "Now, let's see, what would be the best light," she said as she floated from one side to the other.

"How are you doing that?" Spenser asked her.

"Magic," she said, winking at him. "I can control the weather and air elements, so I use them to help me float."

"Wow, can you teach us?" Jackson asked.

The girl's face scrunched. "Who are you? You don't look the normal folk I see come through here, though to be honest, not many people come through here."

"They're my friends, and they're here to help me find my sister," Ruby said.

Gabriella's eyes widened. "You can talk?"

"Well, of course I can talk," Ruby said and a small huff of smoke blew out of her nose.

"But I can hear you and understand you," Gabriella said.

"It's our stone," Jackson said, holding it up. "When I hold it, we can understand when animals speak."

"Put that away," Spenser hissed at him. "We don't know if she's a friend or not."

"I'm a friend as long as you aren't here to harm the forest."

"We just want to find my sister," Ruby said. "Have you seen a blue dragon?"

"A blue dragon too? This is amazing," Gabriella sighed, "but no, you're the first dragon I've seen. However, I would bet the Shadow King has your dragon."

"He sounds scary," Jackson said.

Gabriella nodded. "He can be. Did you bring knights with you?" She looked around. "Magicians?"

Spenser shook his head. "No one would help us."

"Well, you have me now. If he has taken a dragon, I'll help in any way I can."

The group of five wandered even farther into the forest. Gabriella often summoned some wind to blow aside the leaves at the top, allowing sunlight to filter in and light the path.

"I can feel her," Ruby said. "She's close."

"You can feel her?" Spenser asked.

"Yes, dragons have a sense of each other. We know when another is nearby and as she is my sister, the feeling is even stronger."

Suddenly the sound of thumping reached their ears. Gabriella called on the wind again, and the leaves above parted. The sunlight streamed down, landing on a large tree.

"Look, there's an opening," Jackson pointed to a small dark space at the base of the tree.

As they got closer, they realized the opening wasn't as small as they thought. In fact, it was large enough even Ruby could fit through.

"She must be in there," Ruby said.

"I don't know how well my magic will work inside a tree," Gabriella said. "There won't be much beyond air to work with."

"We have to try," Spenser said, and the group entered the dark space.

6 IN THE HOLLOW TREE

The inside of the tree was a lighter brown than the outside bark and Spenser could see arcs of lines running up and down the walls. "It's like they hollowed it out," he said softly.

As they stepped farther into the tree, a large cage came into view. Trapped behind the bars was a large blue dragon.

"Sapphire," Ruby said and hurried to the metal bars.

"Ruby," the other dragon answered, "You have to get out of here. It's a trap. The Shadow King will be back soon."

"He already is," a deep voice said from behind the group.

They turned to see a tall man dressed all in black with dark hair and golden eyes.

"Ah, another dragon. Now, I can have two in my collection."

"It isn't nice to imprison creatures," Spenser said. "Dragons need to be able to fly, and this cage is much too small for her."

"Well, that's just too bad," the Shadow King laughed.

Spenser looked to Gabriella. "Can't you help us?"

"I'll try," she said, "but I think lightning would work best in this situation, and I'm still working on it."

"You can do it," Kayleigh said and smiled at her.

"Thanks, little one," Gabriella smiled back. She closed her eyes and held her hands apart as if holding an imaginary ball. At first nothing happened, but then tiny blue sparks began to shoot out of her hands.

"What is she doing?" the Shadow King yelled. "Stop it."

Gabriella continued to concentrate. Beads of sweat began to form on her brow and run down her face. Suddenly, a bright white light shot out of her hands toward the cage. The force sent

Gabriella back against the wall, and everyone closed their eyes against the flash of light.

"I'm free," Sapphire said happily.

"No, what have you done?" the Shadow King cried, sinking to the floor.

Kayleigh slid off Ruby's back and walked over to the Shadow King. "We saved dragon. You not nice. Why you take her?"

"I just wanted a friend," the Shadow King said. The words came out muffled as he had his hands pressed over his face.

"You can't steal things and expect to make them your friends," Jackson said, also climbing down off the dragon.

Spenser joined his brother and sister. "Yeah, the way you get friends is by being nice to people. You have to treat others the way you want to be treated. Would you like it if someone locked you in a cage?"

"No, I guess not," the Shadow King said sadly. "But no one ever wants to come in the forest because it's so dark. I just wanted someone to talk to."

Gabriella rose from the floor, rubbing her aching backside. Her energy was drained, but she managed to stumble over to the group. "I live here in the forest, and I'll be your friend, but only if you promise to be nice from now on."

The Shadow King's face lit up. "You will? I promise to do my best to be nice."

"You can start by apologizing to Sapphire," Gabriella said.

The Shadow King's shoulders drooped with guilt. "I'm sorry for dragon napping you," he said.

Sapphire glared at the Shadow King, and her large nostrils flared as if she were thinking about spewing fire on him anyway, but after a moment, she relaxed. "I accept your apology, and I'm glad you have found a friend. It is awful to be alone."

"That lightning you cast was pretty cool," Jackson said looking at Gabriella.

"Yeah, but it wore me out," she said. "Sapphire, would you mind taking me back to my home?"

"Of course," the blue dragon nodded and lowered her neck so that Gabriella could climb aboard.

"What about me?" the Shadow King asked.

"You are welcome to come," Gabriella said. "I just need to rest, and I was hoping maybe I could sketch the dragons before you both left." Her voice lilted up at the end as if asking a question.

The dragons agreed and the Shadow King climbed up on Sapphire's back beside Gabriella. Spenser, Jackson, and Kayleigh climbed back up on Ruby's back, and the two dragons led the way out of the cave and back toward the front of the forest where they first met Gabriella.

Gabriella showed them her home, a small hut nestled among a grove of trees. After grabbing her sketch pad and charcoal again, she sat on a stump and sketched the two dragons. When she was finished, Spenser, Jackson, and Kayleigh bid farewell to Gabriella and the Shadow King.

As Ruby and Sapphire exited the forest, they took to the air and flew back to the castle. Merlin stood in the courtyard, pacing back and forth nervously. He turned to face them as the dragons landed.

"Where have you been?" he asked. "We've been worried sick."

"We went to the forest to help Ruby free her sister," Spenser said as he slid off Ruby's back. "Meet Sapphire."

"You what?" Merlin scolded, throwing his hands in the air. "Don't you know how dangerous that is?"

"It was fine," Jackson said. "We met the Shadow King. He was just lonely, but now Gabriella is his friend."

"Gabiewa," Kayleigh echoed and held her hands together like Gabriella had when she summoned the lightning. "Boom. Free dragon"

"Who is Gabriella?" Merlin asked, clearly not understanding Kayleigh's version of the story.

"She's a . . ." Spenser paused as he thought. "Well, I'm not sure what she is, but she can control weather elements, and she helped us in the forest."

"But why didn't you wait for me?" Merlin asked.

Spenser put his hands on his slim hips. "It didn't seem last night like anyone was really excited about helping us, so we did it ourselves."

"We were formulating a plan," Merlin sighed. "You must be careful what you do. You never know when someone might be watching."

Spenser's face wrinkled in confusion. "No one was watching us. No one even knew we were gone."

"For your sake, I hope you're right," Merlin said.

"We'll go do a quick scout," Ruby said. "Thank you for all your help."

"Thank you, Ruby," Jackson said petting her nose. "It was fun."

Kayleigh turned back and hugged Ruby before the two dragons flapped their mighty wings and rose into the air again.

"Come, let's get you home," Merlin said, leading the children back into the castle. None of them noticed the lady hiding in the shadows watching them.

Once they were back in the castle, Merlin led the three children to the throne room where the king and queen were seated on beautiful wooden thrones.

"I see you found them," the king said, rising from his throne.

"Yes, they helped the dragon," Merlin said, "but they came back unharmed."

"That is good to hear," the queen said from her throne. "We thank you. I think it's time to go back home, though. Your mother must be worried sick."

"Well, time is a little different here," Spenser said, remembering his days with the dinosaurs that was only minutes back home. "But yes, we would like to go back home now."

"Yesh, home, pwease," Kayleigh said.

Jackson pulled the stone out of his pocket and handed it to Spenser. "I guess you have to take us home."

"Hold my hands," Spenser said. "Maybe we'll see you again, Merlin."

Merlin, the king, and the queen smiled and nodded as Jackson held onto to Spenser's right arm, and Kayleigh grabbed his left hand. Spenser squeezed the wishing stone and wished to be back home. The room began to fade and the now familiar tingle traveled up his arm. He closed his eyes for a moment, and when he opened them, they were back in his room.

"That was fun," Jackson said. "Let's draw our own dragons."

Spenser had to admit it was fun having his brother and sister along. He grabbed some paper and pencils from his desk and the three children began to draw their dragons as they shared their favorite part of the adventure.

"Hey," Jackson said suddenly. "We never let Kayleigh hold the stone. I wonder what her power is."

"I guess we'll find out next time," Spenser said.

"Next time," Kayleigh said and smiled a big smile.

The End!

Read on for a sneak peek at Book 3

A Look At The Wishing Stone #3 Mesmerizing Mermaids

1 THE BIRTHDAY PRESENT

Kayleigh's birthday was fast approaching and Spenser wanted to find the perfect gift, but he had no money, and she was hard to buy for as her tastes seemed to change by the hour. The only thing he was sure that she still liked was traveling with him back in time and seeing the dragons. She hadn't stopped talking about it since they returned home.

Maybe he could find out what her current interest was and then find a book that would match it. Then he could take her on another adventure. That would be free and fun. He was longing to go on another adventure himself.

As soon as Kayleigh was up from her nap, Spenser rushed into her room to gather his intel*.

"Kayleigh, if you could go into any book, what kind of book would you like to go into?"

Her little face scrunched as she thought hard. "Mermaids. I want to swim and see mermaids."

The answer caught Spenser off guard. He didn't even know she knew what mermaids were, but he would love that too. He loved watching a show on television about mermaids and sometimes he even pretended his legs were stuck together like a tail.

"Okay, I don't have any mermaid books, so we'll have to get to the library again. Let's go ask Mom."

Kayleigh slid off her toddler bed and trundled after him.

"What are you guys doing?" Jackson asked as they passed his room.

"Going to see if Mom will take us to the library," Spenser answered.

"I want to go too." Jackson dropped the truck he was playing with and followed them down the stairs.

Their mom was in the living room, tapping away on her computer. Because she worked all day as a teacher, she often spent afternoons on the weekend working on writing her own books. She claimed she wanted to be a author.

"Mom, can we go to the library again?" Spenser asked, tapping her on the shoulder.

"Again? We just went last week."

"I know, but we need a new book. Kayleigh wants one about mermaids."

"Oh, she does, does she?" Their mother glanced at her screen and then back at the children. A small sigh escaped her lips, but she smiled. "Okay, I would never want to stop the love of reading. Let's go to the library."

After piling in the SUV, the four headed to the local library.
It was becoming a regular stop for them, and Spenser knew
exactly where he needed to go to find a book that might work.

"Come on, Kayleigh, you can help me pick."

She followed him through the aisles and to the fantasy
book section. Once there, Spenser skimmed the offerings until
he found one close to what he was looking for.

"Here's one about a mermaid finding a rare pearl."

Kayleigh scrunched her nose and shook her head.

"Okay," he turned back to the shelf and grabbed the next
one. "Here's one about a mermaid birthday party. That might
be fun since your birthday is in a few days."

"No, look again," she said, shaking her head.

Spenser sighed and turned back to the shelf. Suddenly, his
hand landed on the perfect book. It had two mermaids and a
merman on the cover. One of the mermaids was following a
giant purple octopus. He flipped the book over and scanned the
back text. "This one is about a mermaid who goes missing as
she follows a giant purple octopus."

"Yesh, that one." Kayleigh smiled and reached for the book, hugging it to her chest.

Read the rest of Book 3 on Amazon or where books are sold

https://www.amazon.com/Wishing-Stone-Mesmerizing-Mermaids/dp/1977604811/ref=tmm_pap_swatch_0?_encoding=UTF8&qid=&sr=

References and Medieval Facts:

1. Food in the medieval times was not drab. Instead it was often spiced with black pepper, cinnamon, ginger and saffron. The use of spices was a sign of wealth and therefore the spices were usually displayed on the table. http://www.medievalists.net/2014/12/medieval-food-taste/

2. Though not all castles had the same layout, some common areas that most had were the keep, the kitchens, the courtyard, and the moat. The moat was a body of water surrounding the castle but it did not have a pleasant smell. A lot of sewage was thrown into the moat with no way to flush it away. http://www.exploring-castles.com/castle_designs/medieval_castle_layout/

3. Dinner often consisted of three, four, five, or even six courses. http://www.lordsandladies.org/middle-ages-food-king.htm

4. We take sleeping in a bedroom for granted now, but in the middle ages, a separate room for sleeping was a luxury that only the most wealthy could afford. Cottagers slept on stone slabs covered with a thin mattress of hay or peat moss. Their one-room cottages were kept warm by an open fire in the middle of the room. In the winter, when all the windows were shuttered, the air was thick was smoke. Dew collected on the thatched roof would drip from the rafters in the morning and when it rained no one could sleep. Small birds, mice, and insects living in the roof would scatter debris down on those sleeping below. And if that wasn't enough, the wind would whistle and moan through the chinks in the walls all night long.

A wealthy landowner or town merchant could afford better accommodations for sleeping. A bed with a mattress, sheets, blankets, canopy, curtains, etc. was the most expensive piece of furniture in most homes and they were often mentioned in wills. Some were so sumptuous and impressive that they occupied a prominent position in the area we would call a living room. This room was the family gathering place, where the master and mistress slept, ate, and worked during the winter. The beds were often very large and the whole family could sleep together. Guests were sometimes offered a spot in the communal bed by the fire. It was not uncommon to visit with your friends while sitting, fully clothed in bed. http://stores.renstore.com/history-and-traditions/sleep-in-the-middle-ages#.WL945jsrLIU

5. A chamber pot is a bowl-shaped container with a handle, and often a lid, used as a portable toilet, especially in the bedroom at night. Variants of this were common in many cultures until the advent (invention) of indoor plumbing. https://en.wikipedia.org/wiki/Chamber_pot Because chamber pots were often thrown out the window, sometimes people walking by would get hit. Men used to walk on the right side of women to protect them from the possibility of getting doused.

ABOUT THE AUTHOR

Lorana Hoopes is an inspirational author who lives in the Pacific Northwest with her husband and three children. She has written three adult inspirational fiction books under The Heartbeats series: The Power of Prayer, Where It All Began, and When Hearts Collide. She is currently finishing the fourth book in the series, A Father's Love. http://bit.ly/Heartbeatcollection. She also has a new adult series Star Lake. When Love Returns released 8/17.

Lorana was inspired to write an early reader series for her son when he began reading and The Wishing Stone series was born. Dangerous Dinosaur http://amzn.to/2sNssL8 is the first book in the series, but be sure to stay tuned for #3 Mesmerizing Mermaid which she hopes to release before the end of 2017!

If you would like to see a sneak peek of Book #3, be sure to click here http://bookhip.com/BQRJAF

Made in the USA
Middletown, DE
31 May 2021